short a, e, i, o, and u

Once upon a Time

by Liane B. Onish

Illustrated by Gioia Fiammenghi

SCHOLASTIC INC.

New York   Toronto   London   Auckland   Sydney   Mexico City   New Delhi   Hong Kong

Once upon a time, a mother and father had two sons. The brothers were named Will and Jack.

"Will! Jack! Time for lunch!" Mom called.

The two boys burst into the room. "Grrr!" growled Will and Jack. "We are hungry bears!"

The boys sat down and found their spoons. Steam rose from each dish.

"This dish is too hot!" said Will.

"This dish is too hot!" said Jack.

Dad said, "Yes, it is too hot. You boys may go out and play for a little bit."

Jack and Will did many things together. What these brothers liked to do best was make up stories.

"Jack, it is your turn. Start a new story," said Will.

Jack began, "Once upon a time, there were three bears. One day, Mom Bear cooked a very, very hot lunch. But it was too hot to eat. So the bears went for a walk."

Will jumped in. "My turn!" he cried. "While the bears were out, a little girl went into their house. The little girl had long, yellow hair."

Jack interrupted. "Let's call her Goldilocks!"

Will said, "Goldilocks is a very good name for a girl with long, yellow hair. So, Goldilocks wanted to eat Dad Bear's lunch. But it was too hot. She wanted to eat Mom Bear's lunch. But it was too cold. Baby Bear's lunch was just right. Goldilocks ate it all up."

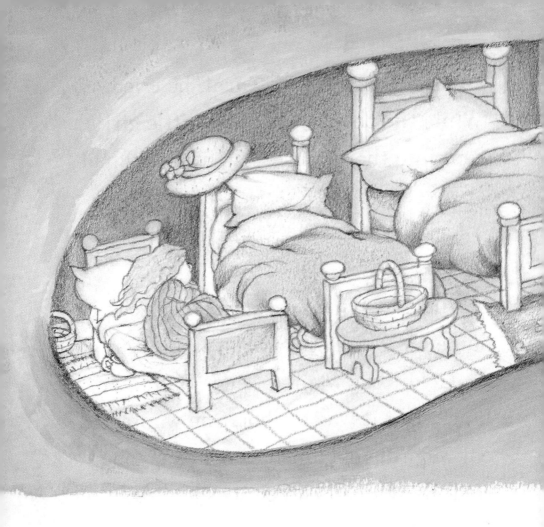

Over their own lunch, Jack and Will told
the story of the three bears. "What
happened next?" Mom and Dad asked.

Jack said, "The little girl sat in all their
chairs. She broke Baby Bear's chair."

Will said, "She sat on all their beds.
Then she went to sleep in Baby Bear's bed."

Jack said, "When the bears got home and saw what the little girl had done, they were mad! 'Grrr!' growled Baby Bear. That woke the little girl up!"

Will said, "She cried, 'Bears! Yikes!' Then she ran all the way home."

"What a good story!" said Mom.

After lunch, the brothers went out to do their garden chores. Jack dug holes in the vegetable bed. Will put in the seeds. Together they picked the ripe, green beans.

"I have a new story," said Will. "It is about a boy and some magic beans."

Jack asked, "Please, can the boy's name be Jack?"

Will said, "Yes, we can call the boy
Jack."

Jack giggled and asked, "And can there
be a mean giant? And a castle in the
sky? And a bag of gold?"

With a smile, Will said, "Yes, our story
can have magic beans, a boy named Jack,
a giant, and a castle in the sky, too."

Will and Jack brought the beans to their dad. They told him their new story. Jack told the part about the castle in the sky. Will told about the mean giant. Then Jack told the part about the bag of gold.

Dad smiled and said, "That's another great story, my sons!" Then he gave them a bag of food for the pigs. "Here is your next job. Please feed the pigs."

The brothers fed the pigs. Then they
watched the animals. One pig rolled on
some straw. One pig slept on some
sticks. And one pig grunted by the rocks.
Will and Jack sat on the fence.

"My turn," said Jack. He began a new
story. "Once upon a time, there were
three pigs. Each pig wanted to build a

house to live in. Pig One found straw. He built his house of straw. Pig Two found sticks. He built his house of sticks. Pig Three built his house with strong bricks."

Will added to the story. "A hungry wolf wanted to eat the pigs . . ."

Just then, Mom called. "Boys, please come here."

"Yum!" cried Jack and Will. Their mom was a great baker. This time, Mom had made a pan of gingerbread men.

Will bit into his gingerbread man.

Jack looked at his. "I think I have another story."

"Tell!" said Will.

Jack said, "Once upon a time, a woman made a gingerbread man. When it was done, she took the pan out of the oven. As she opened the oven door, out jumped the gingerbread man! Then he ran right out of the house!"

"My turn!" Will said. "The gingerbread man ran and ran. As he ran, he said, 'You can run, run, as fast as you can. You can't catch me! I am the gingerbread man.'"

The boys told their story while Mom put some gingerbread men in a basket. She put other food in the basket, too.

"Granny is not feeling well. Please take this basket to her. Remember to stay on the path."

"Yes, Mom," the brothers said.

Along the path they met a girl.

"Hello," Will said politely. "I am Will. This is my brother, Jack. Who are you?"

"Hello," she said. "My name is Rachel, but most people call me Red Riding Hood." The brothers could see why. Red had bright red hair. She wore a bright red cape. Her cape had a bright red hood. "I must go. I cannot be late," she said. "See you!" And off she ran.

By the time the brothers got to Granny's
house, they had a new story.

Granny loved a good story, even when
she was ill. So she sat up in her bed as
Will and Jack told her their new story.

"Once upon a time, there was a little girl
called Red Riding Hood," said Will.

Jack added, "Her real name was Rachel,
but everyone called her Red Riding Hood.
She had bright red hair and she loved to

wear a red cape. Her red cape had a red hood."

Then Will said, "Red Riding Hood went to see her granny. Along the path through the woods, she met a wolf. The wolf wanted to eat her. But when he heard about Red's Granny, he thought he would eat Granny first!"

By the end of the story, Will and Jack's Granny was feeling much better.

At dinner, the boys told Mom and Dad about Granny. They also told their new story about Red Riding Hood.

When the boys were asleep, Mom and Dad sat by the fire. Mom said, "Will and Jack tell very good stories."

Dad said, "Yes, they do."

Mom said, "One day, the boys should put their stories in a book."

Dad said, "Yes! Then we can boast! We will say, 'That book is by our sons, the brothers Grimm!'"

The Grimm brothers were real people. In 1812, Wilhelm and Jacob Grimm published GRIMMS' FAIRY TALES. But the Grimm brothers did not make up the stories in the book. They went all over to hear the stories people told. The Grimm brothers listened and wrote down the stories just the way people told them. The Grimm brothers were the first to put these stories into books.

Which fairy tale do you like best?

23

short a	short e	short i	short o	short u
added	beds	bit	got	but
and	best	bricks	hot	dug
as	end	did	job	jumped
at	fed	dish	mom	just
bag	fence	giggled	rocks	lunch
basket	men	Grimm		much
can	next	his		run
cannot	red	ill		up
castle	them	in		yum
catch	then	is		
dad	tell	it		
granny	well	listened		
had	went	little		
happened	when	pig		
Jack	yes	sticks		
mad		this		
magic		Will		
pan				
path				
ran				
sat				

Phonics Reader 48 ★ Words to Remember

brothers   live   own   time   upon

Phonics Reader 48 ★ Story Words

gingerbread   sons   stories   vegetable